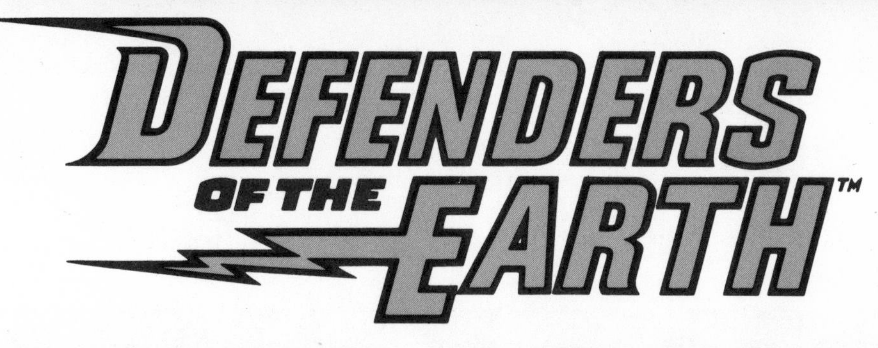

COMPUTER CHECKMATE

Written by William Hansen
Illustrated by Fred Carrillo

A GOLDEN BOOK • NEW YORK
Western Publishing Company, Inc., Racine, Wisconsin 53404

 Library of Congress Catalog Card Number: 86-80135. ISBN 0-307-11766-9/ISBN 0-307-61766-1 (lib. bdg.)
A B C D E F G H I J

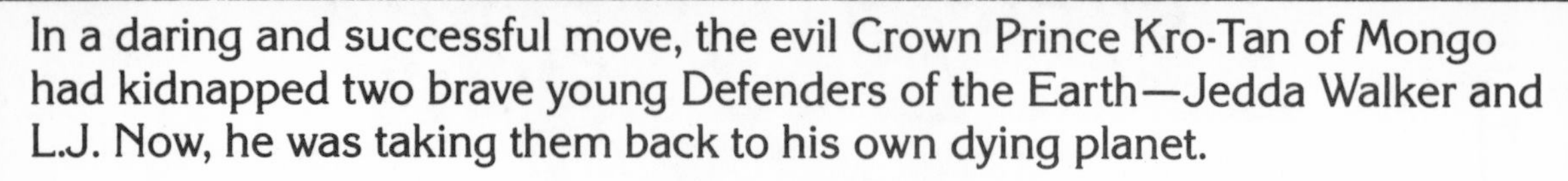

In a daring and successful move, the evil Crown Prince Kro-Tan of Mongo had kidnapped two brave young Defenders of the Earth—Jedda Walker and L.J. Now, he was taking them back to his own dying planet.

Straining against her chains, Jedda said, "If my father, the Phantom, only knew about this..."

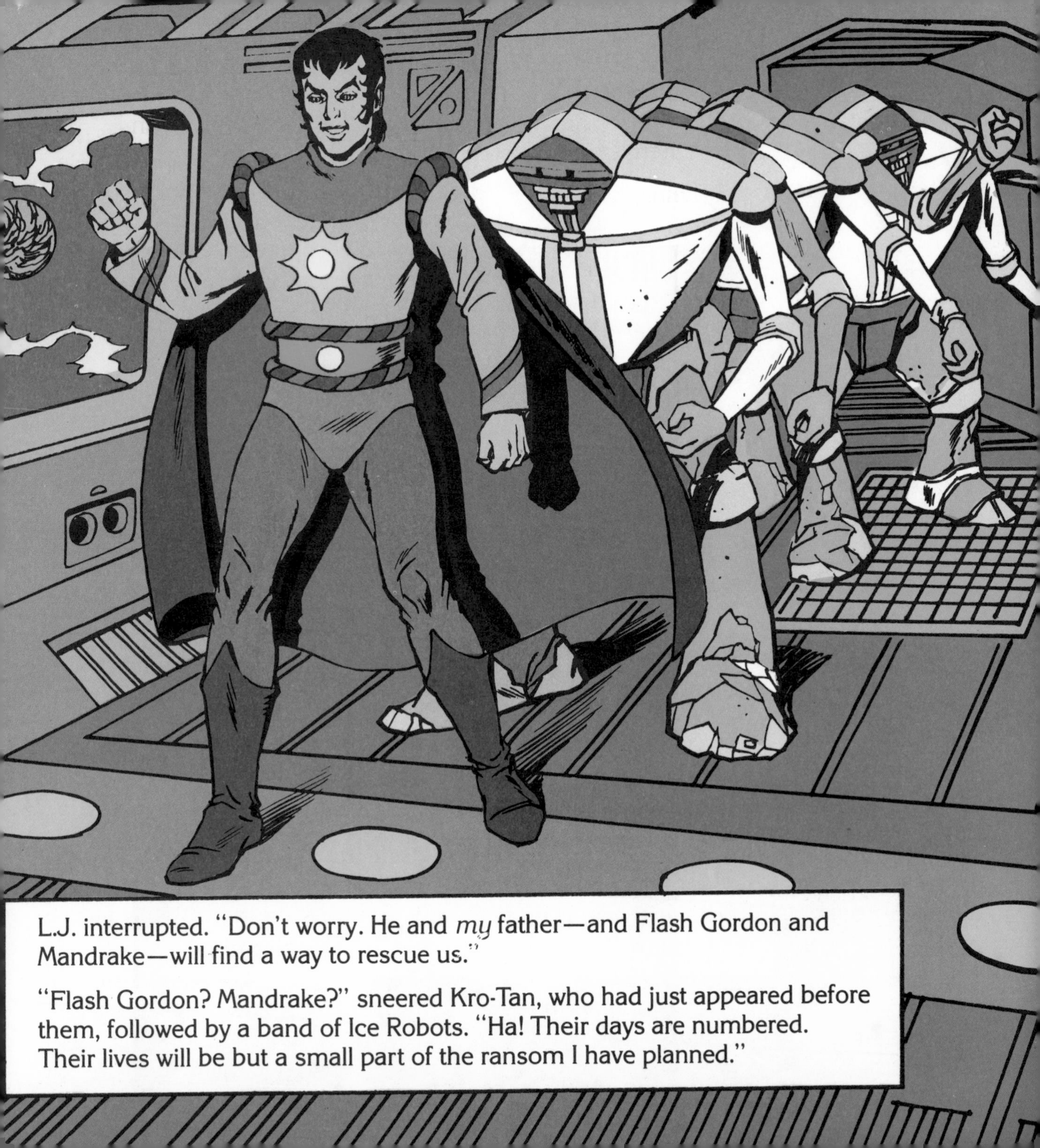
L.J. interrupted. "Don't worry. He and *my* father—and Flash Gordon and Mandrake—will find a way to rescue us."
"Flash Gordon? Mandrake?" sneered Kro-Tan, who had just appeared before them, followed by a band of Ice Robots. "Ha! Their days are numbered. Their lives will be but a small part of the ransom I have planned."

Several times the treacherous Kro-Tan tried to overthrow his father, Ming the Merciless, who had overthrown *his* father. Each time, however, Kro-Tan failed. He had to succeed this time. And he was counting on the cooperation of the great but wicked computer, Octon.
As the spacecraft prepared to land on Mongo, Kro-Tan thought, "Once Octon sees that I have those two brats in my grasp, he will surely help me take over Mongo—and Earth!"

Leaving his prisoners on Mongo, Kro-Tan returned to Earth, and entered Ming's Antarctic headquarters—Ice Station Earth.

With Ming asleep, Kro-Tan stole into the throne room and addressed his father's computer. "Your talents have been wasted in the service of my blundering father. Under me, your true genius can be reached. Together we can rule the universe."

Although Octon had often advised Ming to kill his dishonest son, the computer was impressed with Kro-Tan's move. Octon answered, "Perhaps you are right. Ming *has* been too unsure of himself. What is our next step?"

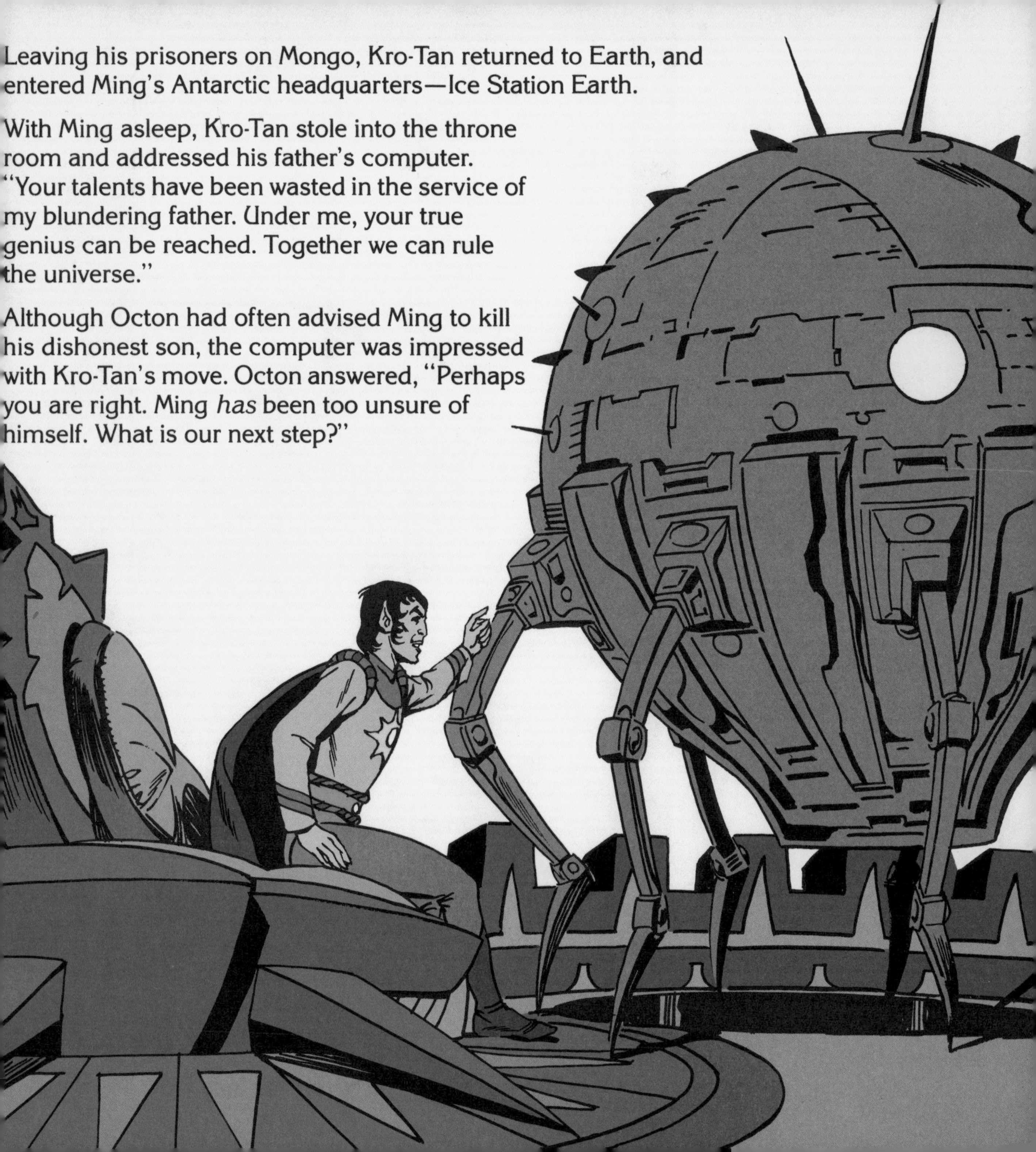

"I want you to challenge Dynak X, the Defenders' somewhat less than perfect computer, to a game of chess," said Kro-Tan. "Tell her that if she loses, she must shut down Monitor's defense systems for twenty-four hours."
"And if she doesn't accept the challenge?" said Octon.
"If the Earthlings have any second thoughts about accepting, remind them about my two young...visitors."

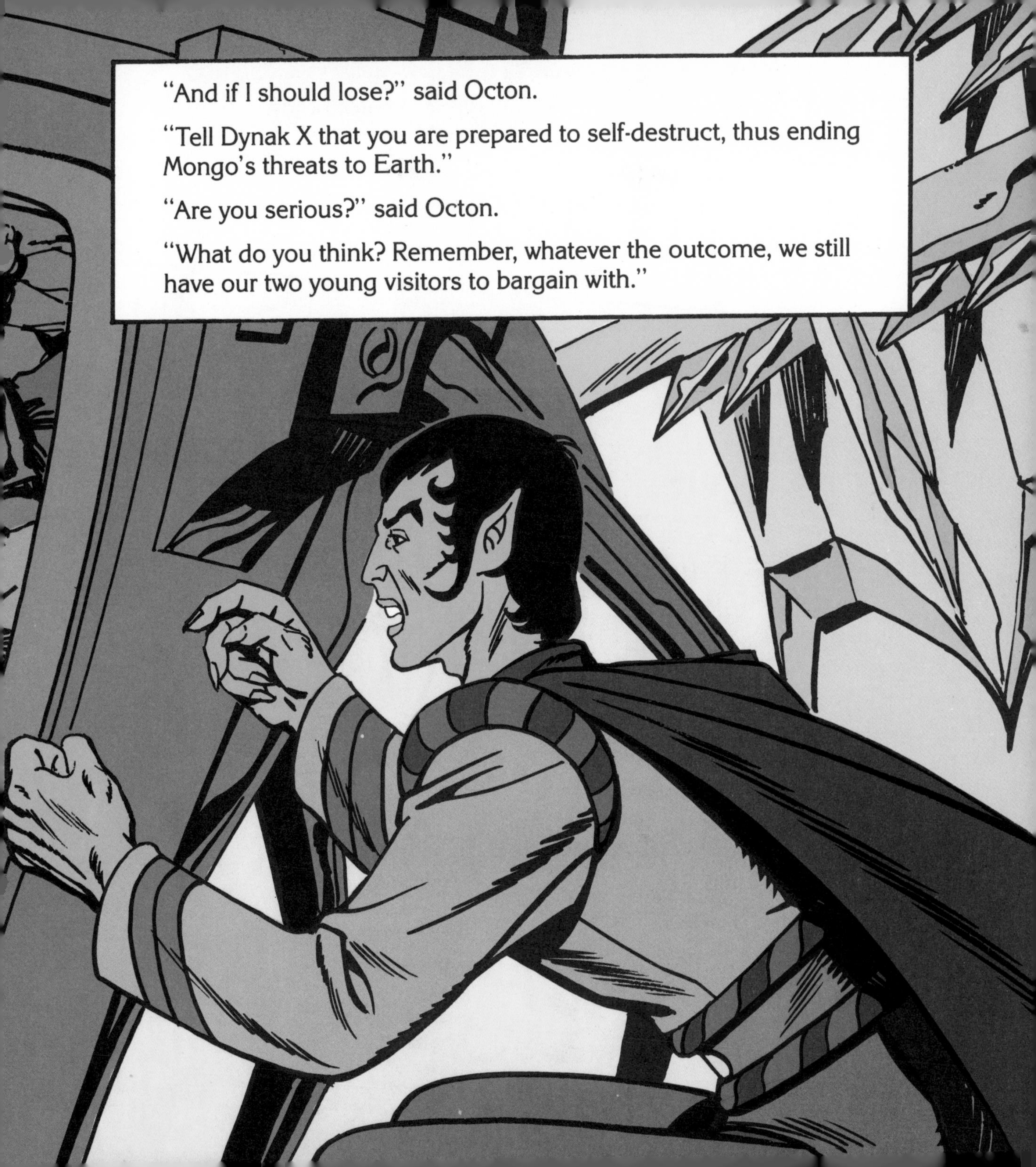
"And if I should lose?" said Octon.
"Tell Dynak X that you are prepared to self-destruct, thus ending Mongo's threats to Earth."
"Are you serious?" said Octon.
"What do you think? Remember, whatever the outcome, we still have our two young visitors to bargain with."

Back at Monitor, the secret headquarters of the Defenders, Flash Gordon, the Phantom, Mandrake, and Lothar were all gathered around the computer screen of Dynak X.

"Here's a message," said Rick with alarm. He relayed Octon's challenge and the news of Jedda and L.J.'s capture.

"Jedda and L.J. must be returned," said the Phantom, "and Earth must be saved. But what if Dynak X loses?"

"If any harm comes to my son..." said Lothar.

Flash said, "I'd like to know why Kro-Tan seems to be in charge. What has happened to Ming?"

"Ah, Octon," said Kro-Tan with glee. "The Defenders have accepted, as I knew they would. Dynak X has sealed the deal by computer honor. How easy it is to outwit those Earthlings. I will have them at every turn. This is fun!"
"Before I start my game with Dynak X, I will make sure your father is kept otherwise busy," said Octon, "lest he interfere."

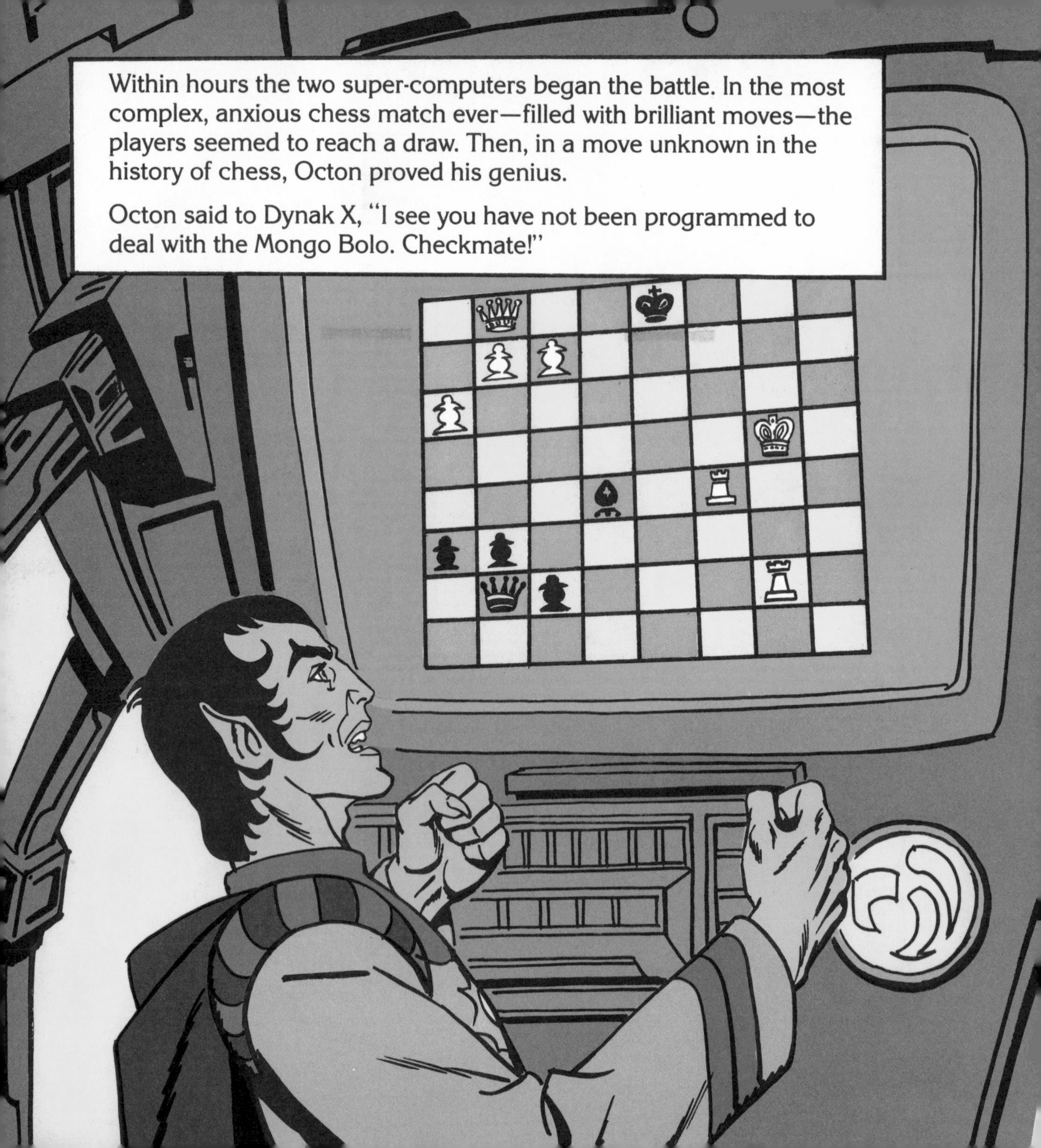
Within hours the two super-computers began the battle. In the most complex, anxious chess match ever—filled with brilliant moves—the players seemed to reach a draw. Then, in a move unknown in the history of chess, Octon proved his genius.
Octon said to Dynak X, "I see you have not been programmed to deal with the Mongo Bolo. Checkmate!"

Dynak X answered, "What kind of move was that? Can it be true? I am finished!"

I CAN'T BELIEVE IT!
IS EVERYTHING LOST?
NOT YET IT ISN'T.
Kro-Tan, delighted with Octon's victory, heaped praise on the evil computer. "Yours was a victory to end all victories. Now your powers shall know no bounds!"

Knowing that he had only twenty-four hours to conquer Earth, Kro-Tan wasted no time. He called on Garax, the leader of the Ice Robots, whom he had persuaded to help him, much as he had persuaded Octon.
"Prepare your robots for invasion," Kro-Tan said to Garax. "Earth will soon be ours. Let us first attack Central City—and the Defenders' Monitor headquarters!"

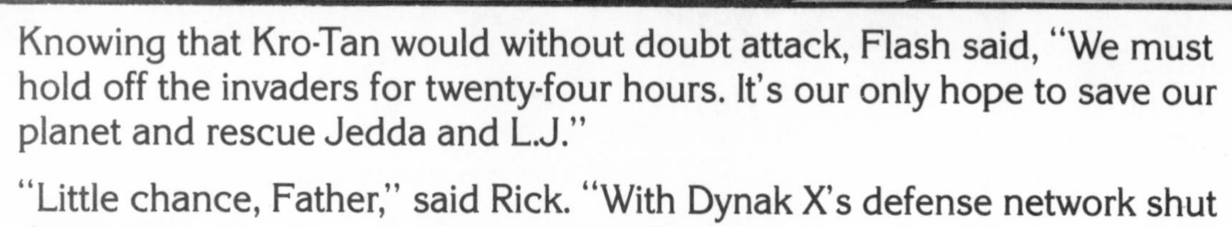

Knowing that Kro-Tan would without doubt attack, Flash said, "We must hold off the invaders for twenty-four hours. It's our only hope to save our planet and rescue Jedda and L.J."

"Little chance, Father," said Rick. "With Dynak X's defense network shut down, we cannot use our weapons with any success. It will take a miracle to prevent Kro-Tan's forces from gaining a total victory."

With Kro-Tan's robot force on its way from Ice Station Earth, Mandrake worked a splendid feat of magic. He created an illusion of another Earth, at a safe distance away from the real one. He made the real Earth invisible to the invaders.

Kro-Tan's army flew completely off course. When they were above what they thought was Central City, they began their attack and destruction... of NOTHING!

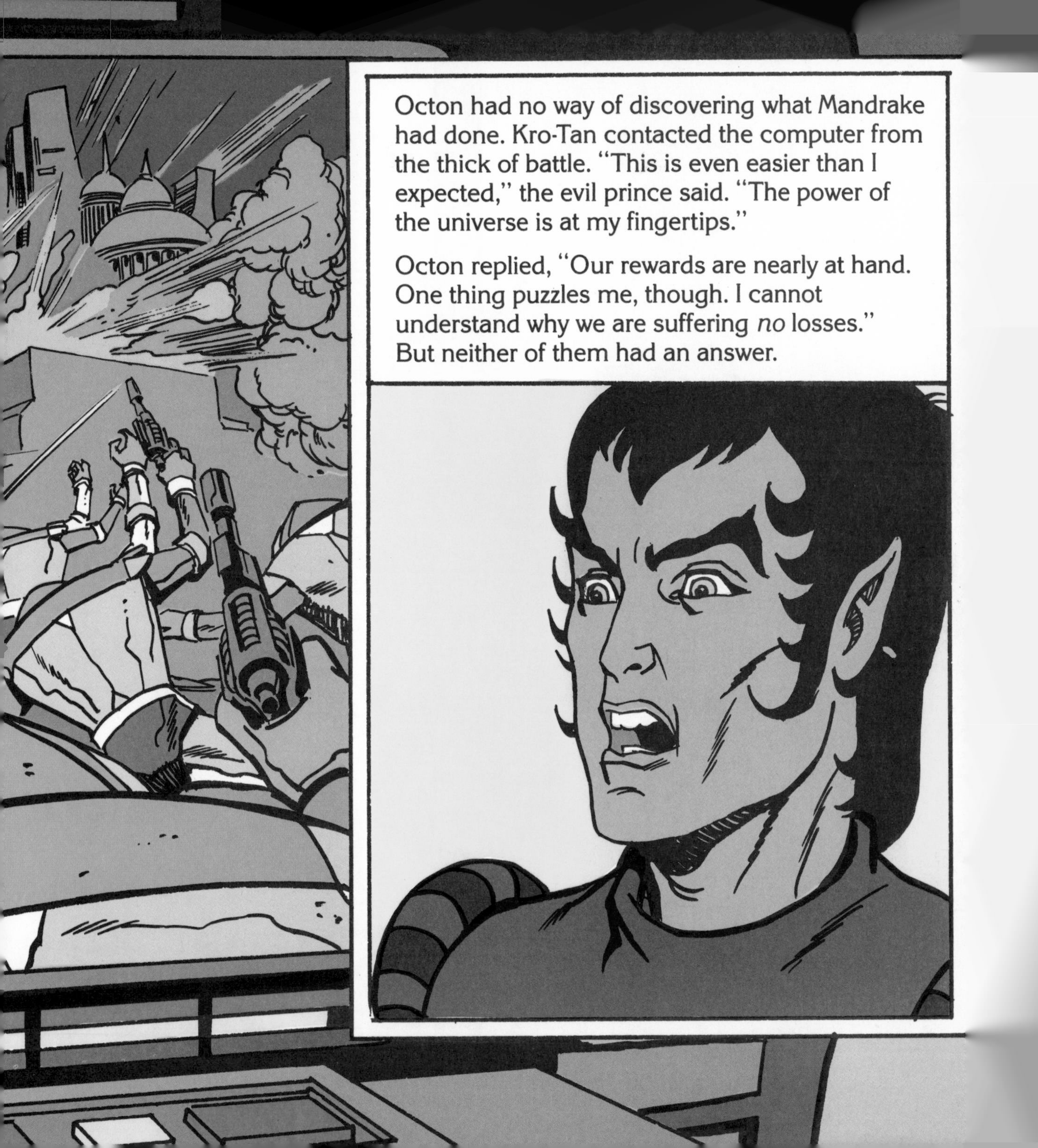
Octon had no way of discovering what Mandrake had done. Kro-Tan contacted the computer from the thick of battle. "This is even easier than I expected," the evil prince said. "The power of the universe is at my fingertips."
Octon replied, "Our rewards are nearly at hand. One thing puzzles me, though. I cannot understand why we are suffering *no* losses." But neither of them had an answer.

Time passed slowly as the Defenders watched the battle Kro-Tan's army waged on the fake Earth. Seconds after the twenty-four-hour period was over, Rick reactivated Dynak X's defense network. The first thing he did was to locate Jedda and L.J.

"We must beat Kro-Tan back to Mongo," Flash said. "We have to free Jedda and L.J. before Kro-Tan finds out his 'victory' is meaningless."

"No problem," said Rick. "We should have enough time, with Mandrake keeping the illusion going."

Landing on the planet Mongo, the Phantom led the way to the icy cavern where Jedda and L.J. were being held prisoner. Calling on the power of ten tigers, the Phantom knocked down the prison entrance and rushed to his daughter's side.
"Father, it's been terrible," Jedda said.
"Wow, gimme a break, Dad!" said L.J. "Where have you guys been?"
"Let's save the talk for later," Flash said seriously. "We'd better be long gone when Kro-Tan gets back here."

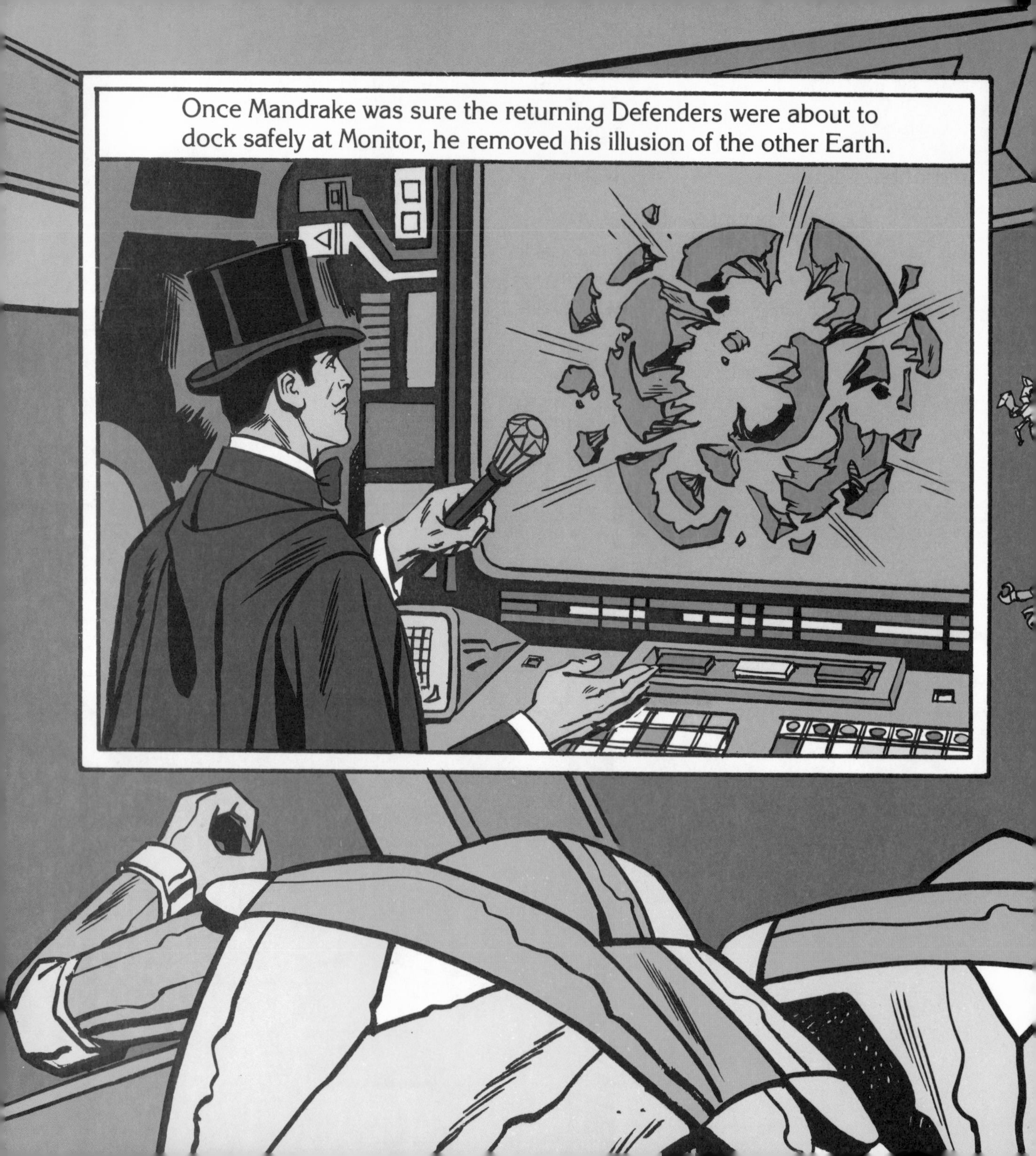
Once Mandrake was sure the returning Defenders were about to dock safely at Monitor, he removed his illusion of the other Earth.

Most of the Ice Robots were stranded in space, and went floating about out of control. Kro-Tan and Garax, who had been observing the battle from inside a spacecraft, were able to get away.
"What happened?" Kro-Tan roared into the communication link to Octon. "Where did Earth go?"
"There have been some problems beyond my programming abilities," said Octon. "Most unfortunate, indeed."
"Idiot computer," said Kro-Tan. "My father will reduce you to rubble!"

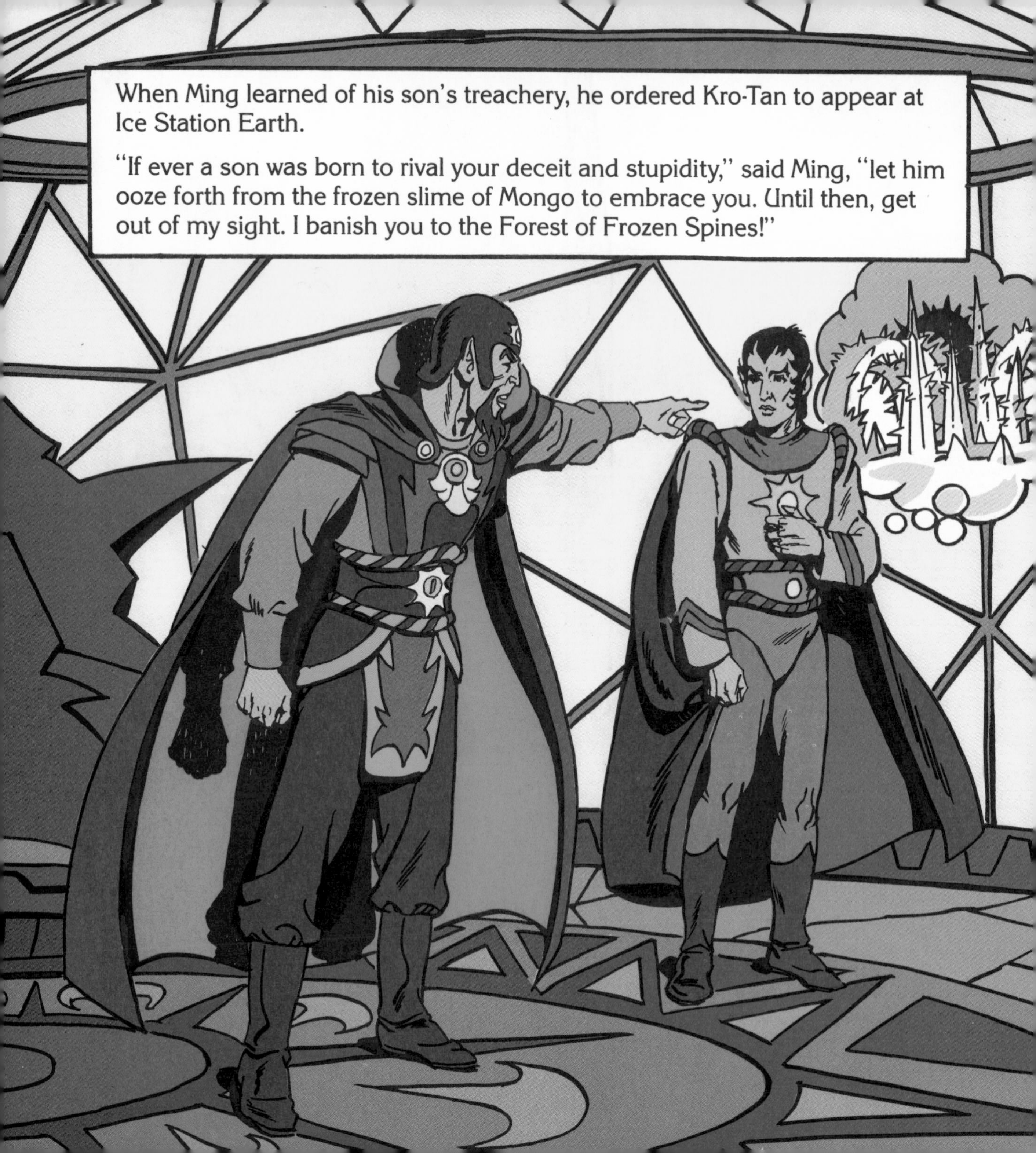
When Ming learned of his son's treachery, he ordered Kro-Tan to appear at Ice Station Earth.
"If ever a son was born to rival your deceit and stupidity," said Ming, "let him ooze forth from the frozen slime of Mongo to embrace you. Until then, get out of my sight. I banish you to the Forest of Frozen Spines!"

Turning to Octon, Ming said, "As for you, my useless bucket of bolts, it's time to say 'good riddance.' My disgust for you knows no bounds."

Octon replied, "May I point out, most merciless Ming, that I have done nothing more than honor the imperial commands of the imperial son of the imperial ruler of Mongo."

Back at Monitor, the Defenders were celebrating.

"Talk about close calls," said Rick.

"Mandrake," said the Phantom, "you've never been more brilliant! I have you to thank for my daughter's return."

"And I," said Lothar, "for my son's."

"Well, Dynak X," said Flash jokingly, "did you learn anything from this experience?"

"Yes," said Dynak X. "I learned never to get hit with the Mongo Bolo again!"

"Checkmate!" said Flash with a grin.

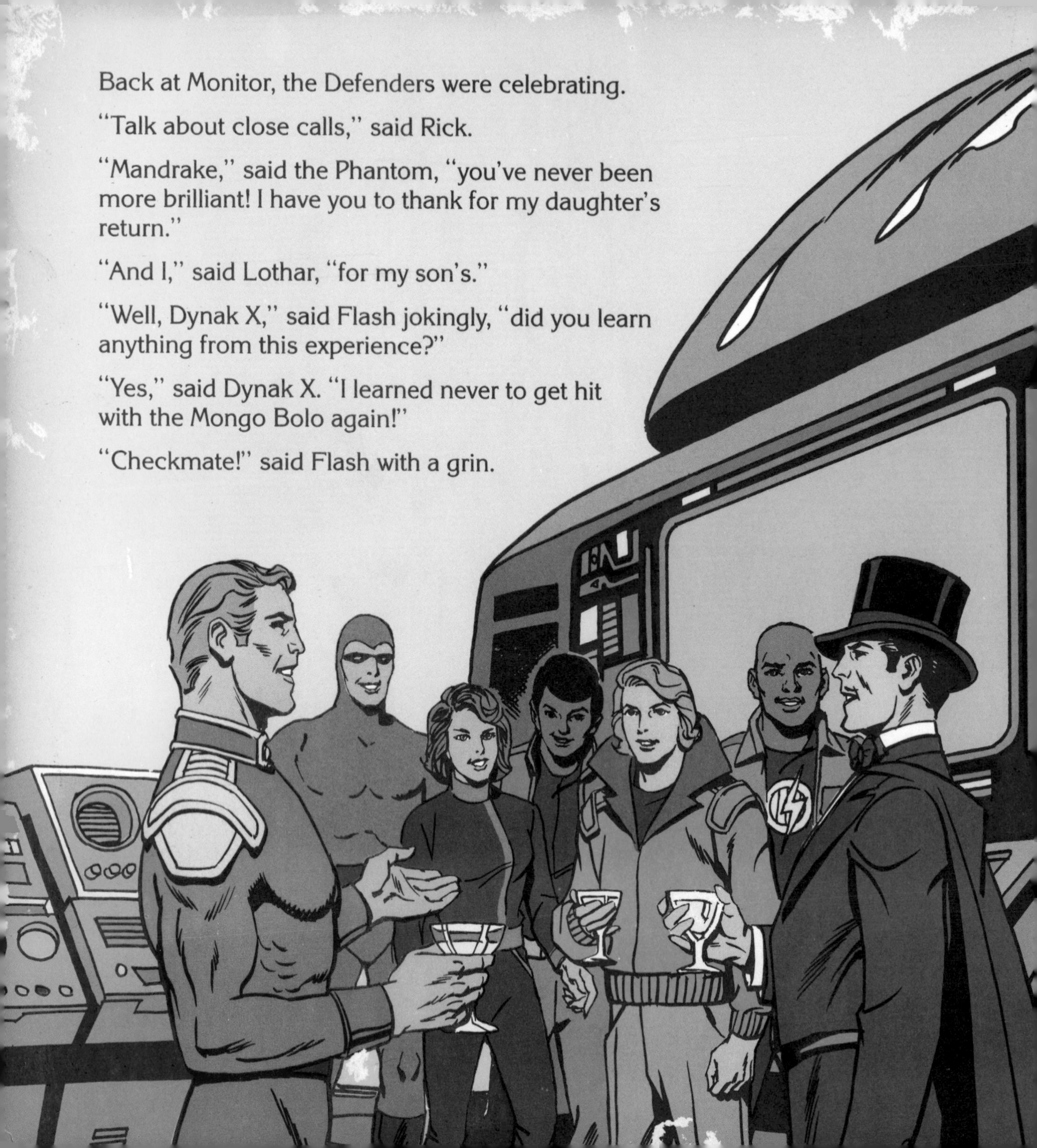